PUMPKIN DAY, PUMPKIN NIGHT

BY
Anne Rockwell

PICTURES BY
Megan Halsey

WALKER AND COMPANY
NEW YORK

For Christian, D.A.N.N.Y., Ting-Ting, and Soyung. —A.R.

For my terrific friend Winky. —M.H.

First published in the United States of America in 1999 by Walker Publishing Company, Inc.

Published simultaneously in Canada by Fitzhenry and Whiteside, Markham, Ontario L3R 4T8

Library of Congress Cataloging-in-Publication Data

Rockwell, Anne F.

Pumpkin day, pumpkin night/by Anne Rockwell; pictures by Megan Halsey.

p.   cm

Summary: Relates a boy's excitement in buying the perfect pumpkin and then making the perfect jack-o-lantern.

ISBN 0-8027-8696-0 (hardcover). —ISBN 0-8027-8697-9 (reinforced)

[1. Pumpkin—Fiction.   2. Jack-o-lanterns—Fiction.]   I. Halsey, Megan, ill.   II. Title.

PZ7.R5943Pu 1999   98-48370

[E]—dc21   CIP

                                          AC

Book design by Sophie Ye Chin

Printed in Hong Kong

2 4 6 8 10 9 7 5 3 1

I know it's pumpkin time
when leaves turn red, yellow, and orange.

The squirrels know it's pumpkin time, too,
and collect seeds and nuts in their cheek pouches.
They're getting ready for winter.
They know that when pumpkin time comes,
winter can't be far away.

At school, we draw faces on paper pumpkins
that we cut out of orange construction paper.
We write our names on them.
We tape our paper pumpkins to the classroom window
so everyone walking past my school will know
that pumpkin time is here.

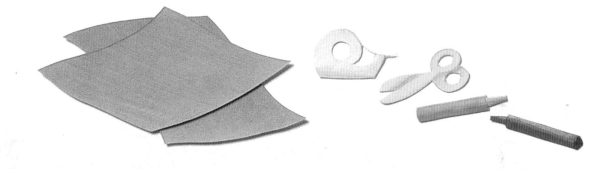

At home, I draw more pumpkin faces.
Some look like this—and some like this.
But I've decided I like the one
with the biggest, widest grin the best of all.

Finally it's pumpkin day!
My mother and I get in the car
and drive to the farmer's market.
Baskets overflow with ears of Indian corn.
There are apples, too,
that smell crisp and tangy-sweet just like fall.
The same old scarecrow stuffed with straw
lies sprawled exactly where he was last year—
across the big pile of pumpkins!

There are so many of them—more than I can count.
I don't want just any pumpkin, though.
No, I want a pumpkin that is as big and round
and orange as a setting sun.

This pumpkin is too tall and skinny.

This round one still has patches of green.

This is the biggest pumpkin I've ever seen.

It is big and round and orange,

but I think it's much too big to be my pumpkin

for it won't even fit in our car.

These are the smallest pumpkins I've ever seen.

"Oh, look, Jeffrey!" my mother says as soon as she sees them.

"Look at these cute little pumpkins."

"I think those pumpkins are much too little to be my jack-o-lantern,"
I shake my head and say.

"But they're not too little for pumpkin pies," my mother says.

"The little ones are the sweetest ones of all."

And so she buys ten of them.

But I don't want ten little pumpkins.

I just want one big one.

So I look some more.

And then suddenly—hiding behind the scarecrow—

I see it! I see my perfect pumpkin!

It is on the grass,

where it had rolled away from all the others.

I think it was waiting there just for me.

I hold my perfect, round, orange pumpkin
carefully on my lap going home in the car.
Beside me in a paper bag are my mother's ten little pumpkins.
"I can't wait to get home," I say.
"Neither can I," she says with a smile.

I sit at the kitchen table
and carefully draw a face on my pumpkin.
I copy the picture with the wide, wide grin.
My mother cuts into the top with its sturdy stalk.
She makes a circle cap that comes off
and fits neatly back on my pumpkin.

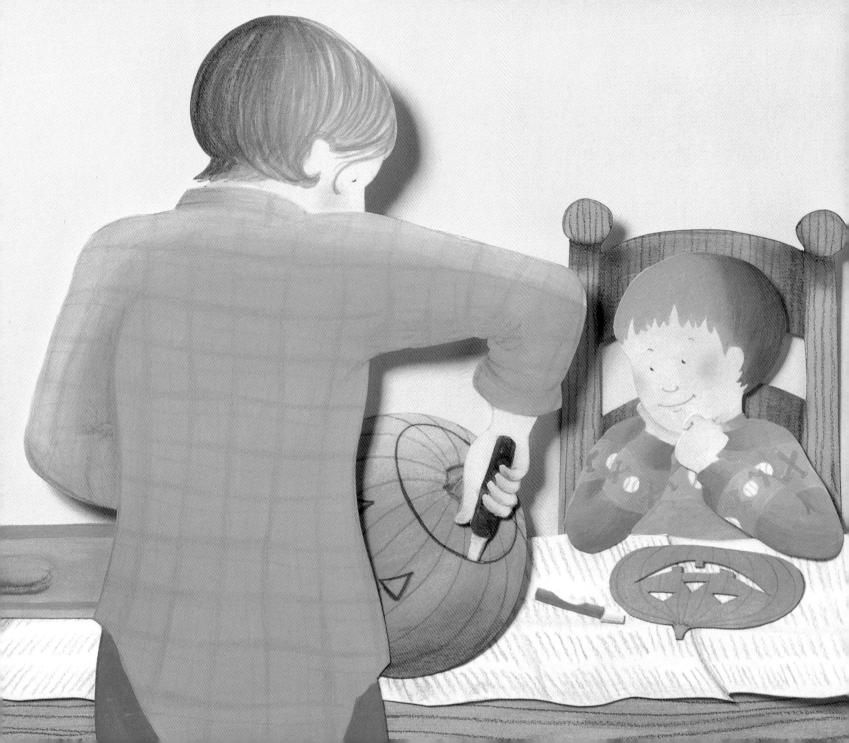

I scoop slimy seeds from inside the pumpkin.
I put them in a pan and sprinkle them with oil and salt.
My mother roasts them in the oven
along with the ten little pumpkins for pumpkin pie.
The kitchen begins to fill with a nutty, yummy smell
while my mother carves out a face on my pumpkin
exactly as I drew it—
with the grin exactly as wide as I wanted it.

While we wait for the little pumpkins to finish baking,

my mother and I put on warm jackets and go outside.

I carry my pumpkin to the old cast-iron table

next to the porch swing and set it down.

I put a fat candle inside where the seeds used to be.

My mother lights it.

As soon as she does,

my pumpkin has a mysterious, grinning glow.

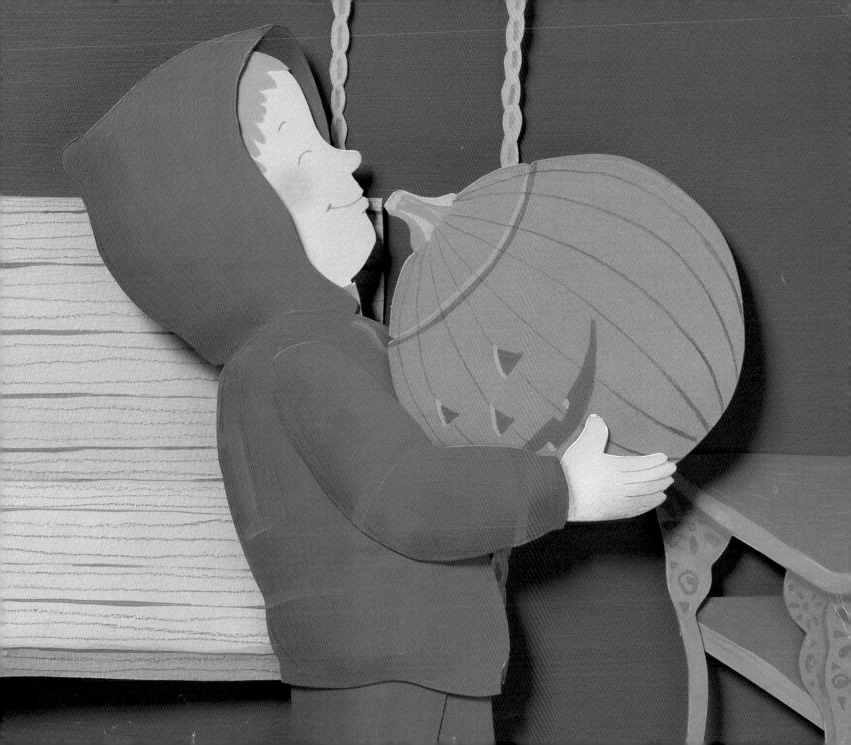

"Jeffrey, that's the greatest jack-o-lantern
I've ever seen," my mother says.
I smile because I know that what she says is true.
I watch my pumpkin glowing in the night.

Almost all the leaves have blown away.

The trees stretch their bare, black limbs across the sky.

I can see every single star up there, I think.

"Look, Mom," I say. "The stars are so bright!"

The stars in the sky are very bright, that's true.

But they're not as bright as my pumpkin!

It glows a fiery orange on a dark and starry night.

My perfect pumpkin grins at the big round moon
white and bright way up in the sky,
while all the little pumpkins turn to pie.